KNIGHTS
OF SUBURBIA

P.A. Kurch

An imprint of Enslow Publishing

WEST **44** BOOKS™

Please visit our website, www.west44books.com.
For a free color catalog of all our high-quality books,
call toll free 1-800-542-2595 or fax 1-877-542-2596.

Cataloging-in-Publication Data

Names: Kurch, P.A.
Title: Knights of suburbia / P.A. Kurch.
Description: New York : West 44, 2019. | Series: West 44 YA verse
Identifiers: ISBN 9781538382738 (pbk.) | ISBN 9781538382745 (library
bound) | ISBN 9781538383377 (ebook)
Subjects: LCSH: Children's poetry, American. | Children's poetry, English. |
English poetry.
Classification: LCC PS586.3 K654 2019 | DDC 811'.60809282--dc23

First Edition
Published in 2019 by
Enslow Publishing LLC
101 West 23rd Street, Suite #240
New York, NY 10011

Editor: Caitie McAneney
Designer: Rachel Rising

Photo Credits: Cover JamesBrey/E+/Getty Images; Cover, p.1 (knight)
Samantha DeMartin.

Printed in the United States of America

CPSIA compliance information: Batch #CS18W44: For further information contact
Enslow Publishing LLC, New York, New York at 1-800-542-2595.

For Sophia

Before the War

my family and I
considered our lives
normal.

That's not to say
that we considered our lives
abnormal

after the war.

It's just that
before the war,

life

was as normal
and stable

as any
normal and stable

(messed up!)

American family life
could possibly be.

There Was

dinner
at six o'clock
every night.
And there was
no excuse
for coming home late.
     And there were
definitely
     no video games
          before homework.
There were
chores to do!
     And there was
church!
Every. Sunday. Morning.

There was
absolutely
     no fighting
       and *definitely*
          no swearing
and there was
     NO WAY
     us three kids
were *ever*
going to listen
        to any of this.

          That house
          was *our* world.

Don't Ask Me How

my dad raised
the three of us
alone.

Don't ask me how
the three of us
survived
under his rule.

When your dad
is the

KING

who oversees
  every school
in the land,
you can't get away
with skipping *class*
or *detentions*.

My dad. Dr. Knights.
Superintendent.

Don't ask me how
he ever survived *us*.

This Was Me

Henry Arthur Knights,

being of
sound mind and body,

acting how any
17-year-old
in my position
would act:

              Like an idiot.

This was us.

Me and my
        twin sister,
Helena Amelia Knights,
both making that

Earth-shattering transition

from teen-hood
              to adulthood.

(I just happened
        to shatter the earth
              harder than she did.)

This Was Us

Me, Helena,
and my
        older brother,
                        Simon.
My
sister and I
are *Honorary Knights*—
both adopted
when we
        were two.

My dad
raised Helena
        and me
        as his own.

(*Mrs. Knights*
        passed away
right after
        the adoption
                was finalized—
        he never
forgave her.)

So,
that made
        two mothers
                I never
                got to know.

My Best Friend

Matthew Holbrook,
once asked
me and my sister
how much
of our
birth mother
we remember.

And the
answer was:
                    Nothing.
We were
too young.

Simon
overheard this,
and he told
me and Helena
that we were
lucky
that we still
even had a mother
            somewhere
                out there.
                        And my dad
                told us
                that *one day*
                        Helena and I
                        could go
                            and find her.

Over the Years

my dad
tried *so hard*
to find us
a suitable mother.

It never quite
worked out.
Because *usually*
one of his
girlfriends
        would leave
        the house
                in a huff.
Because Simon
would fill
their purse
with shaving cream.
Or write
        text messages
to them
from my
        dad's phone
that read:

I can't
wait for you
to meet my wife!

                (Simon was a *monster*.)

Let's just say
my dad's
last date
was a year ago.

Over the years,
I think
my dad
always thought
that our family
was touched
by an extra light.

And
you know what?

Maybe we were.

But when the war,
which had always seemed
to be there,
heated up,
that light
started to fade.

All we could do
was watch.

Helplessly.

(It's the
        same thing I did
when my grades
        in school fell.)

For Months

my dad
had been
talking about
maybe running
for town board.

One night,
he discussed it
with Grandma Knights,
who reminded him
how he once
threw up
during a
college debate,
losing the election
(and his girlfriend).

*Yeah, but this time
will be different,*

he told her.

And for months,
the war overseas
continued
to rage on.

Until,
one day,
it got worse.

This Was Him

My older brother,
Simon Vincent Knights IV.

Football star and
homecoming king.

>After two years
>of college,
>Simon became
>an EMT.

Two years
after that, he quit.

>The war
>had gotten
>too bad for him
>to ignore
>any longer.

This was him:
Doing what our dad
always taught us to do.

To stand up
>*for what we thought*
>>*was right.*

So Simon willingly
and *maybe even
somewhat stupidly*
volunteered
for the army.

I Had Learned

from the best.

Simon
had left home
and high school
a pranking legend.

After all,
he had been
the one
responsible
      for filling donuts
      in the teacher's lounge
      with mayonnaise
and for putting
confetti
onto every
ceiling fan
in the auditorium.

He was
the MASTER
of pranks.

            And I
            would make
                  my brother
                     proud.

When Simon

went off to war,
we all
grew sadder.
        Quieter.
               And I hated it.

When Simon
went off to war,
    I decided
      that pulling pranks
        in his place
would maybe
lighten the mood
a bit.

So I did.

The Pranks

at home
were pointless,
because my dad
was beginning
to spend
more time
at work
        instead of
        at home.
                With us.

So
what else
could I do
except focus
on school?

I Began

to do *anything*
that would get
my dad's attention.

But it usually
only caught
the attention
of Principal Stevenson
and *every*
guidance counselor
in school.

Glue
in the soap dispensers.

       Goldfish
       in the school pool.

They told my dad,
but he would
brush it off.

       So I stopped
       for a while

to think of
BIGGER PRANKS
that he

           couldn't ignore.

As the Months Passed

we waited
for every phone call
or email
or letter
from Simon—

anything
to know
that he
was okay.

As the months passed,
we learned
that his
best friend,
who grew up
down the street,
had died
when his
helicopter crashed
during a sandstorm.

The months passed
and we didn't
hear from him
much more

after that.

A Package from Simon

arrived one day.
The box
was covered
in postmarks
from around the world.

Inside
were pictures
for my dad
of Simon
in hard-to-say places.

For me
there was a green
army Jeep cap
that Simon knew
I always wanted.

And for Helena
there was a copy of
the army newspaper
Stars and Stripes.

The Front Page

is all
my sister
had to see,
after she had
asked us:

Who still reads
the newspaper?

Helena shrieked—
scaring my dad
and making
me swear.

Right there,
on the
front page,
was Simon.

Standing outside
the army
field hospital
where he was
now stationed.

And standing
next to him
was a celebrity
news reporter
who met with him
for an interview.

My Sister's Hero

Gracie Lyn Mahdavi.

Pictured with
    her *other* hero,
        Simon.

You could see
the stars
in her eyes!

Gracie Lyn
was a literary
rock star
to my sister.

And because
Gracie Lyn
just happened to share
the same religion
as those
we were currently
        at war with,
some people
hated her.

            But not
              my sister.

Gracie Lyn was
(and still is)
Helena's hero.

Two Years Later

Simon
finally
came back home
for good.

Our last name,
KNIGHTS,
was boldly stitched
on his uniform.

And my brother!

                            Thinner, older,
                                  sunburned.

He tried
so hard
to be *happy*.

But it became clear,
very quickly,
that he just
wasn't the same.

2 a.m.

is when his
nightmares started
(well, for us,
     at least.)

Simon woke up

SCREAMING,

scaring us all.

At 2:30,

we sat around
     the kitchen table,
          half-asleep,
    realizing that
    unseen wounds
can run
pretty deep.

       For seven days,
       Dad *told*
          my brother
          to get help
             until, finally,
         Simon
          packed his things.

Startled

when the
doorbell rang
one afternoon.

We had
basically been
on lockdown
by that point
(for the family's sake).

I found the door
already open.

And on the porch
was Simon

and *Gracie Lyn Mahdavi?*

Both smiling.

And three of them
crying.

Three?

I was
startled
when I
saw the baby

in Gracie Lyn's arms.

When We Got Home

I went right
to bed.

In a panic.

I wanted
to tell someone.

But everyone
was sleeping.

When we got home,
        my own
nightmares began.

            Sometimes
                        I saved Simon
                        from jumping
            but sometimes
                        I couldn't.

And sometimes
I was thinking
that I was
        losing
                my mind.

Clara Rose

was not
making my life
any easier
as the days
went on.

If my nightmares
         weren't enough
                  to keep me up,
then the cries
         of Clara Rose
certainly were.

As was
the constant
baby talk
from my dad.

And Helena's
endless reading
of *Hamlet*
to the baby
during breakfast.

Simon
and Gracie Lyn
seemed to
encourage
the craziness.

I Couldn't Stand

another minute
in that house.

> My dad
> who normally loved
> *being normal*
> seemed to love
> *the chaos*
> that now
> *consumed*
> our lives.

> And Simon
> was acting like
> *nothing happened*
> on the bridge.

I kept quiet.

> And I started
> wishing
> that I never
> had this family.

But
when I thought that,
I couldn't stand
the guilt

> that came over me.

Sometimes,

I would see
my dad's eyes
well up
with tears.

          I don't think
          anyone else
          ever saw it.

Sometimes
it was when
he was holding
Clara Rose.

          Sometimes
          it was when
          he and Simon
          were arguing
          about *something*
          stupid,

like
good doctors
      or parenting styles.

Sometimes,
my dad
would snap
at any
one of us.

          Sometimes
             he apologized.

                    Sometimes
                    he didn't.

31

Sometimes,
Helena would sit
on the hill
in our backyard
late at night.

The stars
      and the
      city skyline
               in the distance
    sparkled
in the dark.

Sometimes,
Gracie Lyn
would go
and join her.

      And they'd talk.
               For an hour.

And
my sister
would *always*
tell Gracie Lyn
just how much
she wanted
to leave this place.

Sometimes,
my brother
wouldn't just
go outside.
      He would
          sneak outside.

To the side
of the garage.

        And smoke.
              And drink.

Sometimes
for hours.

And I'd hear
my brother,
late at night,
stumbling
as he came back
into the house.

I always
kept my
mouth shut, though.

                    And I shouldn't have.

When Nobody Else Was Listening

I'd hear my dad
on the phone,
        asking my grandpa
about elections
and campaigns.

I'd hear Gracie Lyn
        yelling at Simon
for smelling
        like alcohol.

When nobody else
was listening,
        I would hear him
        promising her
to get help.
        To get better.

Sometimes
he'd yell
right back,
        waking up Clara Rose.

And then
the fighting
would get
        even worse.

On a Good Night

I'd hear
the two of them
singing Clara Rose
to sleep.

And then,
I'd hear my brother go,
   Say goodnight, Gracie,
to which Gracie would reply,
   Goodnight, Gracie.
And they would laugh.

On a good night,
we might all
play video games
or watch
movies together,
and things
would just

   barely

be okay.

  Because,
  on a good night,
  I would forget
     about the bridge.

One Bad Night

I kept dreaming
about Simon
jumping
from that bridge

and I woke up
in a cold sweat.

       I couldn't
get back
       to sleep.

One bad night,
I went outside

where I knew
my sister
and Gracie Lyn

would be sitting.

And they
invited me
to join them.

Gracie Lyn Told Us

all kinds
      of stories.

About college
and her first job
at a *very boring*
paper company

          in Pennsylvania.
          And how it led
          to a job
          at a newspaper.

Gracie Lyn
told us about
beautiful places,

      destroyed by war.

Stories
about her and Simon
falling in love.
          And stories of how
          she was now falling
          out of love.

She told us
how her
own family
      hated her
for getting pregnant.

37

And sometimes
how people
hated her
because she was
Muslim.

(To which
she laughed:
*I was born
and raised
in Atlantic City!*)

As bad as life
seemed to get,
Gracie Lyn told us
to always
keep smiling
and keep
moving forward.

But then
she cried
and got *stuck*

on Simon.

I Wanted

so *badly*
to tell her
about that night
with Simon
on the bridge.

But instead,
my sister and I
told Gracie Lyn
how we imagined
our real mother.

And Gracie Lyn
smiled
as she listened.

Surely,
our mom was
        beautiful.
And funny!
        A world-class cook
and, who knows,
maybe a
world-class
pianist, too.

I wanted
        so badly
        for all of that
to be true.

The Three of Us

jumped
to our feet
when we heard
somebody
by the side
of the house.

Simon appeared
in the dark
and Gracie Lyn
asked him
what he was doing.

And then
he started swearing

at the
three of us.

My Dad Threw Open

the sliding-glass door.
He had his
          bathrobe on
and my
          baseball bat
                    in hand.

He breathed
          a sigh of relief

when he
saw that
it was just *us*.

And then
he realized
that Simon
was drunk
or high.

And my dad
lowered my bat

                    and angrily
                    told us
                    to get inside
before any
of the neighbors
saw or heard.

Things Were Tense

after that.

>Well,
>more tense
>than usual.

During dinner
a few nights later,

>>Simon
>>told my sister:

>>*Put your stupid book down.*

Helena
always read
at the table.

>We had always
>>*accepted* it.

She told him no,
so Simon
grabbed her book

and THREW IT

>>>into
>>>the living room.

My Sister

SNAPPED.

To this day,
        we don't talk about
        that night.

Angrily,
she admitted
        how sometimes
        she wished
Simon *never*
        came home.
And how much
        she was looking forward
        to finding our
real family
        when she and I
turned 18
        because *clearly,*
this family
        was screwed
and any family
        would be better
than the idiots
        sitting
        in front of her here.

That Night

dinner ended early.

           The dishes
           did *not*
           get washed.

        My dad
                once again
        disappeared
                to his office.

Simon
took off,

        while Helena
        and Gracie Lyn
                went upstairs.

                                To pack
                                their things.

They stopped packing
when I told them
about Simon
nearly jumping
from the bridge.

        My sister
        felt *horrible*.

           And Gracie Lyn
           was crushed.

Helena and Gracie Lyn

both *agreed*
that I should
tell my dad
about Simon
and the bridge.

Helena
and Gracie Lyn
went downstairs
with me.

We knocked
on my dad's
office door.

Nothing.

We knocked
a second time
and a third time.

He told us
to go.

And leave him
alone.

On the Last Week

of school,
I tried everything
to get myself
suspended.

Just to see
    if my dad
    would *even notice.*

Things
did not go
as planned.

On Monday

my teacher
had asked me
to share my
experiences
with the class
about being adopted.

So I said to her:

Well, Miss DeLellis,
given my current
situation at home,
I would say
that being adopted
flipping* sucks.

(*Henry Arthur Knights
doesn't use the word *flipping*.)

Get Back to Class

Mr. Knights,
and don't let me
see you in here again,

Principal Stevenson
told me.

Aren't you going to
                call my dad?

            I asked him.

Surely,
swearing
at a teacher
was grounds
for suspension.

But Principal Stevenson
just told me
to *get going.*

So I did.

And I felt
so *defeated.*

On Tuesday

Matthew and I
staged a fight
in the parking lot.

Nothing.

On Wednesday,
I found out

that my dad

would be
visiting our school
on Friday
for the
end-of-the-year
assembly.

This was
        too good
to pass up.

Operation Round Table

was a prank
that *everybody*
in school
was talking about
by Thursday morning.

No one knew
when
or *where*
it was going to happen.

And no one knew
just *who*
was behind it.

They wrongly
assumed
that the
senior class
was responsible.

Because I'm sure
                    my brother's
        past senior pranks
were still

fresh

in everyone's minds.

That Afternoon

all the teachers
and counselors
and Principal Stevenson
were nervous.

On Friday morning,
the school auditorium
was set
for my dad's
arrival.
      And (I swear!)
          every teacher,
          gym coach,
              janitor,
              librarian,
                  and counselor
                      was marching
                the halls
            just waiting
            for any sign
        of Operation
        Round Table
      to begin.

At 9 a.m.

Principal Stevenson

regretfully

announced
over the
loudspeaker

that Superintendent Knights

would NOT
be visiting us
today.

And then
he called me
          and my sister
to the office.

My Dad

was sitting at
Principal Stevenson's desk
when I walked in.

My sister
was standing
right next to him.

She looked sad.
                    Upset.

My dad
kindly asked
Principal Stevenson
to give us
a few minutes.

And
Principal Stevenson said,
Of course,
and he patted
my shoulder
as he closed
the door
behind him.

Dad Looked Hurt

but not angry.

He told me
that Simon
was arrested
that morning.
                    My heart sank.
And my dad
broke down
in tears,
telling us
that Gracie Lyn
just told him
about what happened
on the bridge.

I told him:
            I wanted
                    to tell you.
            I would have
                    told you sooner.
                        But I
                    was too scared.

And Then

our dad
admitted
that he too
had been scared.

Scared
after finding
drugs
and empty
beer cans
in the garage.

Scared
that Simon
was getting
even worse.

And then
my dad
told us
to keep a secret:

Knight's Honor.

A World of Trouble

is what
he said Simon
was in.

That morning,
Simon
had shown up
for work
at the hospital
very drunk.

He was in
a world of trouble,

because at the
police station,
Simon got
into a fight
      with *two officers*

        and Gracie Lyn.

So We Gave Him Time

to sober up.

We gave him time
to sit there
in a jail cell.

And we
gave him time
to *really consider*
just how much
he truly
needed help.

He was back home
that day.

We gave him time
to apologize.

And then
Gracie Lyn
gave him

a piece

of her mind.

Her Response

to Simon's
       stupidity
       (her words, not mine)
has become
a Knights
family legend.

Because
the second *after*
Simon finished
       apologizing
              to us,
                     Gracie Lyn
                     told my brother
                            to *go outside.*

Simon
looked terrified.

The Four of Us

Me, my dad,
Helena, and Clara Rose
pretended like
we weren't listening.

And honestly,
we couldn't *hear a thing*
from inside.

Helena
peeked first.

And then
        I followed.

And my dad,
holding Clara Rose,
        followed *us*.

And
the four of us
stood there.

Our noses
pressed against
the glass door.

I Think She's Gonna Hit Him

Helena said,
as she
carefully studied
Gracie Lyn's
movements.

And my dad laughed,
    saying:
        She's not gonna hit him!

And then
Helena replied:

No... I really think
    she's going
        to hit him!

And Like a Bolt of Lightning

Gracie Lyn

STRUCK!

slapping Simon
across the face.

Like a bolt of lightning,
my dad
covered up
Clara Rose's eyes.

And like a bolt of lightning
all four of us

disappeared
in a flash.

That Night

Simon
came up to my room
and knocked
on my door.

I told Simon:

Please don't tell me
            we're going
                    for another walk.

Simon swore
        and shook his head.
And then
he sat down
        at my desk
                and apologized
for everything.

And
that night
he promised
to make it up to me.

Somehow.
                Knight's Honor.

During Dinner

my dad
asked me
what this
Operation
Round Table thing
was all about.

And he knew
I was the one
behind it.

C'mon,
       he said.

Knights? Of the
         Round Table?

And I told him
that Operation
Round Table
was *literally*
nothing.

Because sometimes,
     the best prank
        is *no prank*
            at all.

With a Mouthful

of food,
Simon
nodded his head
in proud,
brotherly approval.

At first,
my dad
didn't say anything
as he
thought about
what I said.

And then,
with a mouthful
of food,
my dad
nodded his head, too.

Rumors Travel Fast

even in a big
suburban town.

Rumors of
Simon's arrest
had become this

incredible story!

Complete with
      a high-speed
           police chase
                and the stealing
                   of an ambulance.

      Rumors of
           a local journalist
      living with the
           Knights family

and rumors
of my dad
      quitting
           the school board
      to run
      for town supervisor

were traveling

fast.

Team Effort

is what
my dad
said we needed
to win
the election.

One other person
would be
running against him.
But my dad
wasn't worried.

My dad also
wasn't worried
about stepping down
from the
school board soon.

I guess
I wasn't
too happy
with the idea
of spending my
summer vacation
going door-to-door
to hand out flyers.

                    And put up posters.

          But at least
                    I'd be *outside*.

The Gears

started turning
in my head.

(And there was
            no stopping them.)

My ideas
were *almost*
as amazing
as the waffles
that morning.

I raised
my glass
of orange juice
and made
a toast
to team effort!
                (To the surprise
                        of the whole family.)

Simon smirked.

He knew
something was up.

The Next Morning

I watched
the local news
as I ate
my cereal.

And then,
it hit me.

The answer!

To my
master plan.

My dad
couldn't ignore

this.

The Town Board

had willingly
and maybe even
        somewhat stupidly
agreed to spend
        half a million dollars
on a new
video scoreboard
for the town
        football field
at Prospect Park.

(My dad
        was *strongly* against
                such a waste
                        of taxpayer money.)

But to me?

That
very expensive
new scoreboard
wouldn't be
a waste of money

at all.

Matthew Then Told Me

how the
town board
    had asked
    our high school

to spare 20

of their *best*
art and film students
    to make a video
    for that
    new scoreboard.

Something that
town board
    could *proudly* show
    during the big
        Fourth of July
            football game.

And so
Matthew and I
made a visit
to our school
that day.

Maybe

my charm
  or my
  natural leadership
won those
20 students over.

Maybe the 20 students
  who were back in school
during the first week
  of summer vacation
wanted some payback.

And maybe
my idea
  just sounded
like more fun.

So Henry Knights
  bravely
  came to their rescue.

Miss Jill,

the art teacher,
would stop by
the film department.

> Every day
> she told me
> how proud
> she was
>> that I,
>> Henry Knights,
>>> *was volunteering my time*

>>>> for such a
>>>>> patriotic cause
>>>>> (if only she knew).

> This video
> would be her
>> *crowning*
>>> *achievement.*

But we
couldn't show her
anything.

> We promised
> Miss Jill
> that it would be worth
> the wait.

Everyone Told Us

that we needed
       a good distraction
             for the game.
       Just in case
             things get bad.

I told Matthew
to meet me
at the football field
tomorrow.

           I'll bring a whistle.

                You bring birdseed.

Everyone told us
that we
couldn't train
the seagulls
in Prospect Park.

But Henry Knights
and Matthew Holbrook
           did exactly that.

Every Time

I blew my whistle,
Matthew
would throw
    a handful
    of birdseed
        onto the field.

And about
30 seagulls
would swoop down

and eat the seeds.

We did this
over

and over

again.

We did this
every single day
that week

for an hour.

Everybody Came Out

to Prospect Park
to see the game
(and the fancy
            new scoreboard)
that Fourth of July.

Simon
stayed home
with Clara Rose
(I would
        later learn
                that the sound
                        of fireworks
                                scared him
                                        after the war.)
Gracie Lyn,
though,
stopped by
with a news
cameraman.

And the band
started to play
as they marched
onto the field.
            And I froze.

                            The band.
                    I forgot about...

                    THE MARCHING BAND!

75

The Bandleader

blew his whistle

and then,
like *something*
out of a
horror movie,

more than 100 seagulls
        dove down
                onto the field.

The bandleader ran
and the rest
of the band

s c a t t e r e d

while mothers
and fathers

tried to calm
their *screaming*
        children.

The cameraman
filmed
        everything.

Everyone Was Saying

how strange
that was.

Everyone was saying
how *odd*
it seemed
that every time
a referee
blew his whistle,
the birds
came flying in.

The referee
kept looking
up in the sky.
                        In fear.
It was
pretty funny
to watch.

And
once it got dark,
everyone was saying
how *excited*
they were
to see the video
that the
high schoolers
had made.

The Crowd

fell silent
as the video
started to play
on the expensive
new scoreboard.

And then
A DEAFENING BLAST
of patriotic music

(startling
         the crowd)

and pictures
and video footage
of my dad

         (most of it good).

                  And my voice,
                           telling the crowd:

Vote Dr. Simon Knights
for town board
superintendent.

A good man.
A good father.
And a good Knight.

I Then Appeared

on that giant
    500-thousand-
            dollar screen,
wearing my best
suit and tie.

I turned
to the camera.

And
with a smile,
I said:

          Hi! I'm Henry Knights.

          And I approve
          this message.

Everyone laughed
and roared.

And then
came the gasps.

And whispers.

     Some people
       even *cheered.*

My Dad Wanted to Die

right there.
In Prospect Park.
    (*What a way to go.*)

My dad
wanted to kill me!
Right there.
In Prospect Park.
    (*But there were*
        too many
           witnesses.)

My dad
wanted to tell
Gracie Lyn
to tell her
cameraman

to *STOP FILMING!*

But it
was too late.

Dozens of people
    in the crowd
were taking
    selfies
in front of
    the new
    video scoreboard.

He Then

grabbed me
by the neck
of my shirt
      and he told me
      we were leaving.

People pointed
and took pictures
of us.

Now *I*
was embarrassed.

His face
was red.

*I had gone
too far.*

Matthew
must have
seen me
and panicked,

            because he then
            blew *his whistle.*

Everyone screamed
as the birds
dive-bombed
the stands.

We Came Home Early

that night,
and Simon
        jumped off
        the couch
once he saw my dad
dragging me
        by my shirt
        up the driveway.

Simon
was asking
        me,
        my dad,
                anyone

to tell him
what was going on.

No words
were spoken
the night
we came home
                early.

The Investigation

took 20 minutes.

I took
    full
    responsibility.

                    I mean,
                        I had to.

                I approved
                    that message!

Principal Stevenson
yelled at me,
        saying

how unprofessional
        this stunt was,

and how bad

        it made the
the school
        and town look.

The investigation
ended.
                And Miss Jill
                        never talked to me
            again.

83

The Fallout

was worse
than expected.

    Every student
        who had helped me
    now faced
        summer detention
            and I was now
    their enemy.

The school board
had a special hearing
and my dad
wasn't invited.

It was there
where Simon
    started arguing
    with the school board.
Telling them
that nothing
was damaged
        and nobody
        got hurt.

A security guard
threw him out.
        The fallout
        made the news
        that evening.

Our Good Name

was *basically* destroyed.

My dad
was forced
to step down
from the school board
early.

And he wanted
to put *both*
        me *and* Simon
        up for adoption.

        (Second time's
                the charm!)

It seemed like
the end of the road
                for the Knights family.

Grandpa Knights

lived
      in California.
Be he caught wind
of *everything.*

And he invited us
out west.

Grandpa Knights
      promised my dad
      that like anything
      in politics,

the worst
possible things
      are forgotten
      by the public
in a matter
of days.

So you can still
run for office,
      Grandpa Knights said.

And then
Grandpa Knights promised
that everything
would be

okay.

The First Thing

my dad told
Grandpa Knights
was

NO.

He told him
there was
    too much
to deal with
at the moment.

And that his
chances
of even winning
the election now

    were slim.

And the first thing
that Grandpa
said in reply?

But we
already bought
    the plane tickets!

Nobody Was Going

(*Especially* me
　　and Simon.)

My dad
hated the idea
of me and Simon
being
　　rewarded
with time
at the beach.

Because of my
　　stupid prank
　　on July Fourth.

And my brother's
　　stupid shouting match
　　with the school board.

Since he suffered,
we would, too.

Nobody
was going
　　anywhere.
　　　　　　We were grounded.

And Simon said:

　　　　You can't ground me!
　　　　　　I have a kid!

My Sister Begged

and again
my dad said *no*.

She ran upstairs
and just
minutes later
came back
downstairs
with two packed bags.

And Gracie Lyn
was telling
Clara Rose
how beautiful
California was.

And *how nice*
her great-grandparents
sounded.

My sister begged.

And my dad
begged everybody

to stop.

The Doorbell Rang

and Helena,
who was
already sitting by
the front door,
answered it.

She brought in
a package.

Addressed to my dad.

And my dad,
who wasn't expecting
any package,
placed it
on the table

and looked at it
curiously.

He opened it.

And his face
          went pale.

Inside the Box

were 600
        campaign posters
that I had printed
        in a late-night
flash of genius.

And all of them
had my dad's
        picture on it,

printed
with the words:

A good man.
        A good father.
                And a good Knight!

My Dad Slowly

closed the box.

And then,
slowly,
he looked up
and *glared* at me.

                    I took
              a few steps back.

And slowly,
I said to him:

Whatever
you do, Dad,
please.
           Don't.
                Yell.

And then,
he yelled:

QUIET!

    before yelling
    for everyone to hear:

           WE LEAVE TONIGHT!

              I heard Helena
                  shouting for joy.

No More Dirty Tricks

my dad
made me promise
during our
long flight
to California.

I wasn't
completely honest
with him though.

Because
before we left,
I grabbed about
200
campaign posters
from the box

and carefully
packed them
into my bag.

Open Arms

and a
booming laugh.

          That's how
          Grandpa Knights
          greeted us
          at the airport.

Grandpa
messed up
Helena's and
my hair.

He gave
my brother
a fake punch
on the arm.

          And kissed the cheeks
          of Gracie Lyn
          and Clara Rose.

And then
Grandpa Knights
walked up
to my dad

          and put him
             in a headlock.

                    My dad
                begged his father
                    to stop.

As He Drove Us

to the house,
>   Grandpa Knights
>   told everyone how
happy he was
>   that Clara Rose
>   turned out to be
>   so *cute*.

And Helena,
confused,
asked Grandpa
what he meant.

And Grandpa replied,

I was worried!
>   *Your brother Simon*
>   *was such an*
>   *ugly baby!*

My dad protested.
Gracie Lyn laughed.

And
poor Simon
>   just shook
>   his head.

Long Days

at King's Beach

> is how
> *most of us*
> were spending
> our time.

But Dad
and Grandpa spent

long days
at the house

talking about
> voters,
> and money,
> and elections.

Grandma Knights
eventually told them
both to

SHUT UP!

and to save
grown-up talk
for long nights.

By the End

of our sunny
two weeks
in California,

I had posted
                199
of my dad's
campaign posters
in restaurants,
                    parks,
                    supermarkets,
                            and beaches.

By the end
of our two weeks
in California,
some people
were actually
recognizing
my dad!

And he was
so confused.

On Our Last Day

an officer
stopped me
in the airport
when he
caught me
hanging up
my very last
campaign poster.

I was toast.

And my dad
gave me this look.

And he
begged the officer

to put me
on a plane

that would
take me

far, far away.

As Soon As We Landed

my dad
        was *already*
on the phone
        with a campaign manager
(one that Grandpa picked)
        who made *real*
election posters.

And Simon
        was already
on the phone
making an *appointment*
        with a doctor
(one that Grandma picked)
        who worked with
veterans like him.

As soon
as we landed,

life finally seemed
to settle down.

Life Settled Down

because Simon
soon told us
that he was
comfortable
in his
own skin again.

And my
sister and I
were thinking
      that maybe
            we wouldn't
look for our
birth mother
once we turned
18.

Life settled down

until Gracie Lyn
told my dad

that *four* people

were now
running
against him
in the
election.

Within Days

there were
campaign posters
                    everywhere
            that did not
            belong to my
                    dad's campaign.

And Simon
            had a few
                    choice words
with our neighbor
who had just
            hammered
            one of those
                    campaign posters
into his lawn.

They called
            the police
                    on him.

It Only

went down
from there.

Gracie Lyn
started getting
threats at work

because of her
stories
and reports
about the
ongoing war.

Some threats
she was used to.

But *these* threats
were getting
personal.

Simon
heard about them
and he started
drinking again.

And then
Simon
started to skip
his appointments
with his doctor.

I Heard

arguing
and yelling
outside one morning.

My dad
came into the house,
shaking.

He told
Helena and me
not to go outside
today.

        And not to take
        Clara Rose outside,
                either.

Gracie Lyn
sat on the couch
in tears.

I heard
Simon outside,

SWEARING.

Bright Red Letters

were spray-painted
across our
garage door
where someone
had written
the most
hateful things
about Gracie Lyn.

People started
coming out
of their houses
just to see
those

bright red letters.

Simon Swore

at the neighbors
who were staring
at our house
from across
the street.

> *Is there*
> *anything else*
> > *you morons*
> > *would like to see?*

he yelled,

before
kicking
the tires
of Gracie Lyn's car.

The police
were called

again.

The Police

had gotten
to know Simon
pretty well
over those
few days.

And Simon
got to know
the police
pretty well, too.

> Because they
> arrested him
> that morning
> for being drunk
>> and disorderly
> in public.

He needed
help.

> But the police
> wouldn't listen.

I felt
as defeated
as I did
the day
Principal Stevenson
didn't suspend me
for swearing
in class.

As the Days Passed,

we were
all living
          on edge.

As the days passed,
Gracie Lyn
talked about
moving out.

As the days passed,
wc played
with Clara Rose
inside the house
until things
settled down.

And those days,
Simon was
the angriest
I had ever
seen him.

And no one
really blamed him.

It Became Clear

that between
the upcoming election,

keeping
his family safe,

and trying to keep
his eldest son
on track,

that life
was not about
to let up
on Dr. Simon Knights.

It became clear
that we

Knights

might not win
anything.

Shattered Glass

all over
the driveway.

The windows
of Gracie Lyn's car
were smashed
in broad daylight.

Just *minutes*
after she
finished bringing
groceries
into the house.

There was
shattered glass
everywhere.

It looked
like a bomb
had gone off.

Nobody

had seen it
happen.

Or rather,
nobody
was willing
to step forward
to talk about
what happened.

The police
came by,
again.

                They took pictures
                of Gracie Lyn's car.

Asked us questions.

        Made a report.

They told us
all we could do
was wait.

That Day

I promised
myself
        that I would
        never let
                any family
feel the way
that we did.

Gracie Lyn
decided it was
best
to take
Clara Rose
and stay
at a friend's place.

That day,
Simon
started to drink
more than
                ever.

And
that day
would *forever*
change me
and my family.

There Wasn't Anything

that Gracie Lyn
or my dad
could say
or do
to get Simon
to calm down
and stop drinking.

Gracie Lyn
finally left
in anger.

She apologized.

My dad
yelled at Simon:

Just stop!
And come inside.

And Simon
yelled back:
               Maybe I don't
                   want to stop!

And Then

Simon
punched the
garage door
with his fist.

And broke it.

His fist!
            Not the door.

My dad
was furious.

And then
he became
more furious
when he
had to take
        my very
        drunk brother
to the hospital.

And explain
to the
ER staff

how that
happened.

Two Hours

is how long
it took
for Helena and I
to sweep
and vacuum
all the
broken glass
from the driveway
and from the
inside
of Gracie Lyn's car.

          It was
          the least
          we could do.

Two hours
at the hospital
until Simon
and Dad
came home.

Quickly

my dad
said to Simon
as they both
walked up
the driveway.

Not
another word
was said
between them.

I noticed
Simon
trying to hide
his bandaged
left hand.

My dad
threw Helena
his car keys.

And then
he asked her
to bring the car
into the garage.

Quickly.

Dark Gray

storm clouds
began to fill
the sky
        and the drizzle
            of raindrops
became
    heavier.

Helena and I
then realized
that we couldn't
    stay outside
for much
longer.

Lightning
started to flash
within those
dark gray clouds.

Through the Door

I saw
my brother—
a father,
a son,
a soldier.

A beaten man
who felt
(rightfully so)
that the world
was against him.

And through the door
I saw myself
apologize to him
for everything—
for every
   stupid little
word or thing
I ever said
   or did to him.

The Moment

I opened the door,
I heard my dad
shout *something*
to Simon
downstairs.

Simon
was sitting
at the kitchen table
—alone—
and it was clear
he had been
drinking.

The moment
Simon
yelled back
at him

and the moment
          Simon picked up
          his phone

and threw it
at the door
behind us
          is the moment
          we moved
                    very quickly
                            out of the way.

I Looked Down

at his
shattered phone
that now sat
on the
kitchen floor.

And then
I realized
that Helena and I
were *on the floor,*

        too.

              Frozen. In fear.

Simon
then looked down
at us.

     Speechless.

Breathing heavily.

And then
he put his hand
on the back
of his head
and he *laughed.*

We're Over Our Heads

Simon
said to us.

I looked at him,
confused.

> *What?*
> I asked him,
> somewhat angrily.

Simon
then pointed
at me and
my sister,
and he said:

> *We're over*
> *our heads.*
> > *You two,*
> > *especially.*

Helena
shot right back:

Oh, just like
the six-hundred-
> *dollar phone*
> > *you just threw at us?*

Simon Told Us

how our dad
could never
win some
stupid election.

Because *no one,*
he told us,
    votes for someone
who has a son
      that screws up
as much
as he does.

Simon told us
that we
were all stupid
for thinking
that our family
even had
    a chance.

And
he told us
that my
sister and I
were even
more stupid
for thinking
that our
real family
was any better.

As It Turns Out

the mother that
Helena and I
were *planning*
to find
after our
18th birthday
gave us up.

Not because
she *wanted to*
                    but because
                    she had to.

The court
ruled to have us
taken away
because our mother

was an alcoholic.

                    Hey! Just like
                    your older brother,
                                Simon admitted.

And he laughed.

                    You come from
                    two families
                                of screwups.

Helena Ran Outside

in tears,
screaming
and cursing out
everybody.

I stood there,
in pained shock.

Fifteen years!

                Fifteen *years*—

of dreaming about
the perfect mother
we never had—
was gone.

Just like that.

My dad
came running
downstairs,
asking us
just what
in the world
all that yelling
was about.

Simon
told him
what had
been said

and my dad
very gently
told me
to calm down.

And sit down.

And then
he told Simon
that he had
one day
to pack his things.

My chest
was in knots
as I held back
my tears.

It was pointless.

The tears
streamed down
my face.

Thunder
shook the house
and the rain
started to pour.

And that's when
my brother said
that Helena
just took off
running.

I Have Never Seen

my dad
move more quickly.

I have also
never seen
my dad
swear so *much*—

         most of which
            was directed
        at Simon.

My dad
tore apart
the kitchen
looking for
his car keys.

Simon
then reminded
my dad
     that he had
     tossed his car keys
          to Helena
          in the driveway.

Car keys
that she
probably
still had
     when she
        ran off.

And Then

my dad
ROARED
before he started
to chase
my brother
around the house.

They *leaped*
over the
kitchen table
       and the couch
       in the living room.

I could tell
that Simon
was too drunk
to keep running.

And then
Simon
fell to his knees,
begging:

Please!
Just hit me!
      And get it
      it over with!

I Decided

to stop
wasting time
as Simon
and my dad
continued
to fight.

I decided
to get
outside
        before Helena
got any
        farther.

The storm
grew stronger
        and I think
in some ways
I had, too.

The rain
was coming down
in sheets

and thunder
rumbled
in the distance.

What a Mess

I said to myself,
as I maybe,
possibly,
started to have
second thoughts

about going out
into the storm

on foot.

Alone.

And I thought
about how messy
things were.

And
how much
of a mess
would be left

to clean up

once this
storm passed.

The Glow of the Streetlights

reflected onto
the soaking-wet
concrete
beneath my feet.

It was
just about
my only light.

As I started
to run,

        I swear,
        my heart
            was in
            my throat.

The thunder
grew louder.

Closer.

With every
explosion of thunder,

my sister
     felt farther
          and farther

                         away.

I Then Realized

that I had reached
the end of my
neighborhood.

Ahead of me
sat this
new neighborhood
that had only
recently started
to take shape.

About a dozen
half-built houses

lined both sides
of the street.

I then realized
that Helena
could now

      be anywhere.

I started
      to panic.

I Stood There

for only a minute.

I called
Helena's name,
but I knew
she wouldn't
          hear me.

I stood there
as ice-cold
          rainwater
flowed past
my ankles
and into
the storm drains
by the curb.

I stood there.

Wet.
Cold.
Exhausted.

And scared.

I decided
to turn back.

I Ran

as fast
as my feet
could carry me.

My lungs
burned
inside
my chest

and I didn't
stop.

Not once.

A van
approached
from down
the street.
Its headlights
        lit up
        the night.

I heard the van
slow down
as it got closer

and I ran
even faster.

I Have Seen

a lot
of movies.

And
because of that,
      I have quite
            the imagination.

So when that
HUGE VAN

approached me

in the middle
of that rainstorm,

I was not
about to stop!

The van
sped up
and the horn
started beeping.

And then
      I *really*
            took off.

The Van,

of course,
was faster
than me.

I stopped.
       Out of breath.
My heart
       was going
            to explode.

This was it.
       I was dead.
            Kidnapped!
            Murdered!

I squinted
to see
just who
       or what
was inside
the van.

                     My heart
                           was still beating
                           inside my throat.

The passenger door
flew open
and Gracie Lyn
hollered at me
to get in.

Gracie Lyn Told Me

that Helena
came home
just minutes
after I left.

Figures.

Gracie Lyn told me
how she
asked to borrow
          a *newspaper*
                delivery van
when she
remembered
that her car
      was in our driveway
with its windows
smashed out

and how scared
my dad was
when he called her.

And I Told

Gracie Lyn
just *how bad*
things had gotten
in just

the *few hours*

that she
was gone.

I told her
about Simon
breaking his hand
        and the chase
        throughout the house
and everything
about my
real mother.

And
I told her
how grateful I was

that she
came back.

We Went Home

where we saw
two police cars
parked
in the driveway.

Flashes
of red and blue
police lights
lit up
the falling rain.

The police
were arguing
with my dad

          as Helena
          tried
          telling everyone

that Simon
just took off
in our
dad's car.

My Brother

had probably
gone out
to look for *me*.

And we knew
that he was
in no condition
to get behind
the wheel.

We tried
explaining this
to the police,
but they
made it clear
that they
had heard

enough.

The Police Officers

were A:
soaking wet
with rain.

And B: tired of being
called to our house.

And C:
convinced
that we all
sounded crazy.

>My dad
>couldn't keep track
>of which one of us
>was gone.

The police officers
then pinned
my dad
up against
one of the cars
before
reading him

his rights.

Gracie Lyn and I

raced
back to the van

and the tires
squealed
as we sped away.

Gracie Lyn and I
took the
shortcut
to the old
stone bridge.

As we drove,
the rain
slowed down.

And then
so did Gracie Lyn

and I.

The Skies Opened

and that's
when we saw
my dad's car
against a tree.

> The front of it
> was crushed.

Smoke poured
from under
the hood.

> And there
> was Simon,
> sitting against
> the wall
that he once
walked along.

He had
his hands
over his head.
> And he
> was crying.

> And talking.

> To *himself.*

Gracie Lyn
parked the van
> across from him.

And she told me
to stay put.

I Don't Know

what she said
to him.

He looked
at her.

His face
was blank.

His blue eyes
were empty.

His forehead
was bleeding.

He stared
at Gracie Lyn
like she
was some
stranger.

She helped
him stand up.

He looked
lost.

Confused.

Like he
wasn't even
in there.

The Ambulance

arrived within
minutes
of us calling.

As did
the police
and my dad
and Helena.

The EMTs,
some of which
used to work
with Simon,
approached
            their friend
softly.

And then
they managed
to get him
into the ambulance.

It was
the most
painful thing
I had ever seen

but also
the most…
            comforting.

In the Days That Followed

we went to see
Simon
every day
in the hospital.

And my
sister and I
went with
my dad
and Gracie Lyn
when they both
picked up
their new cars.

In the days
that followed,
Gracie Lyn
and Clara Rose
moved back in.

My dad
sat down
with me
and Helena
and he told us

everything he knew

about our mother.

And how
sorry he was
that he
hadn't been
more honest.

*I love you both
very much,*

he would
say to us.

*And you
deserve
to find your mom.*

In the days
that followed,

we grew closer.

And that
made all
the difference.

The Election

was now
just over
a month away.

Now usually,
Grandpa
and Grandma Knights
would come up
the week
of Thanksgiving.

But after hearing
about Simon
and after realizing
how close
the election
now was,

my grandparents
surprised us all

and showed up
at our door
on the first

of October.

Grandpa Knights

called everyone
into the
living room
where he had
        covered
the walls
with election maps
and posters.

And then
Grandpa Knights
gave us this
beautiful speech
on how
we would all
work together
to make sure
my dad
would win.

And after
he was finished,
my dad
said to him,
somewhat sadly:

Did you really
have to put
so many nails
        into my walls?

We Learned

that Simon
was making
the most
of his hospital stay.
   My dad
   would get
   phone calls
   from Simon
  (and nurses)
about his
late-night
hallway parades
   and patient
   parties
   on the elevators
      (the fire marshal
       ended that one
        pretty quickly.)

He was
my brother
again.

   And we learned
   he would
   be home
     on the first of November.

Simon's Jaw Dropped

when he
opened up
his bedroom door.

You couldn't
step one foot
in his room.

Because,
over the last
30 days or so,
Grandpa Knights
had put boxes
(upon boxes)
full of
campaign signs
in there.

And
Simon said:

I could maybe
understand this
        if dad was running
for president.

But seriously?

        All of this?
        For town board?

149

Six Days

before the election,
my dad had the

BIGGEST

argument with
Grandpa Knights.

Our campaign posters
kept *disappearing*
from town.

Grandpa Knights
was getting tired
of spending
money
to replace them.

My dad
told Grandpa Knights:

We didn't need
so many of them
in the first place!

Five Days

before
the election,
my dad
was invited
       to speak
       at this
       big dinner
           in town.

Every
news channel
was going
to be there.

And Grandpa Knights
told my dad
       that all of us
should be there,
too.

My Dad Wasn't So Sure

and he told
Grandpa Knights
that this probably
wasn't a good idea.

And Grandpa Knights
told him:

*Everyone
will adore the kids!*

*What could possibly
go wrong?*

So There We Were

Me,
Helena,
Simon,
Gracie Lyn,
and Clara Rose.

Proud,
but miserable
                    and bored!

With
        awful food
and music
that was
        too loud
for Clara Rose.

There we were,
as cameras
were recording
everything.

And *there I was*
wondering if Simon
            and I
would be able
to keep it all
together.

As Dad Was Interviewed

we, too,
had our moment
on camera.

The children
(and grandchild!)
of Dr. Simon Knights

all there,
at that dinner,
showing their
support for
their father.

Gracie Lyn
knew just about
every reporter
in the room.

As my dad
was interviewed,

Gracie Lyn
called a reporter
over to our table.

And Simon
stood up.

Simon Said:

My father
is a great man
                    and I
                    promise
                    to you all
that demons
will run
                    if he loses
                    this election.

Simon
then stood
on his chair
with Clara Rose,
and shouted:

Give me liberty
or give me death!

The reporters
laughed.

(Simon
            didn't drink *once*
                        that night.)

My Sister and I

tried to get
Simon
to come down

or *at least*
hand us
the baby.

Gracie Lyn
looked right at me,
wondering if
Simon
maybe left
the hospital
too early.

My dad saw us
and I knew
that he
was thinking

the same thing.

Four Days

before
the election,

      the video of Simon
      speaking to the
      reporters

had been
      viewed
            and shared
            more than a
                thousand times.

Grandpa Knights
flipped!

And four days
before the
election,

he asked me
to try and get
that video
          taken
             down.

I told him
the internet

               doesn't work
                like that.

Three Days

before the
election,
my dad's
        biggest opponent,
Tom Austin,

was caught
stealing
campaign posters
        from around
        town
and
throwing
them away.

The mystery
of our
missing posters
was solved.

Dad celebrated!
        And Grandpa snapped:

Tom Austin threw out
        a thousand dollars' worth
                of campaign posters,
                        you fool!

Two Days

before the
election,

Simon
stopped talking
to Gracie Lyn.

When Grandma
asked him why,
he told her
that Gracie Lyn
called his doctor
and told her
that he still
needed help.

*I was
two days away*
        *from finishing
          counseling!*

And Grandma told him
that maybe
it was for
the best.
        *And Grandma
          is always right.*

The Night Before the Election

I heard Simon
and Gracie Lyn
arguing in bed
about which
Ghostbusters movie
was the best.

I heard everything
as my grandpa
argued with
my grandma
about which
color tie
would look nicer
tomorrow.

And I heard
Helena
quietly playing
her guitar.

So I went
and sat with her.

The Next Morning

at breakfast,
my well-rested dad
asked why
all of us
looked *so tired.*

So we explained.

And then
Gracie Lyn
asked him,

> *What's your*
> *favorite Ghostbusters*
> *movie?*

And Grandma
asked him,

> *What color*
> *will your tie be*
> *tonight?*

Helena and I
asked him
for the
correct words
to the
Fuller House
theme song.

And my dad,
surprised,
confused,
and a little annoyed,
put his face
into his hands.

And then,
            my dad asked
            all of us:

                        Just what in the
                            world goes on
                                in this house
                                    at night?!

Election Night

is a
waiting game.

Election night
is kind of like
New Year's Eve
where everyone
sits around
the TV.

        Some
        excited,

             some
             half-asleep.

That's
exactly how
the living room
looked.

Election night,
though, isn't
        as fun.

Because unlike
New Year's Eve,

Election night
has winners
        and losers.

It All Started

at 9 p.m.

The mood was
surprisingly
calm
as family
and friends

gathered in
our living room.

Some had
donated
     lots of money
to my dad's
campaign.
         (And my dad
    and grandpa
       made me
    and Simon
       promise
       not to swear
    around
       ANY of them.)

It all started
slowly.

And then:

The Numbers

started
to come in
on the TV,
        although
        most of us
        were glued
        to the
        news sites
                on our phones.

I was
reloading
the page
        constantly.

Seconds passed.

Minutes.
        An hour.

At 3,000
votes behind,
Grandpa Knights
told my dad
how much
he would like
to stay here
with us
on the East Coast
after the election.

My dad groaned.

At 2,000
votes behind,
Grandma Knights
invited Simon
to stay
in California.

For a few months.

To see a good doctor.

My dad sighed.
        Gracie Lyn cried.

At 1,000
votes behind,
Helena
looked up
from her phone
and told us
(like it was
        no big deal)
that she would
be graduating
from high school
early
to go to college
and study
the stars.

My dad
started sweating.

I looked
at my sister
        in disbelief.

                I heard
                Grandpa Knights
                telling my dad
                not to sweat
                so much.

                        It looks bad, son!

                My dad
                        quietly swore.

        He was now
        only 500 votes
behind.

I Guess

it was now
my turn
to say *something*,
but I guess
I couldn't.

I guess
I couldn't
understand why
Simon
was willing
to leave
again
and why
Helena
was leaving
so soon.

Life
in our
house
had been
so much
better.

I guess
the idea
of losing
them *both*
was too much.

Nobody Seemed to Notice

as Simon
stood up
and walked out
of the room.

Everyone was
too busy
focusing on
those stupid
numbers.

And
because of that,
nobody
seemed to notice
that Simon
had gotten
pretty upset.

        Except me.

Nobody
seemed to notice
as I got up
and followed him.

Outside

Simon told me
as nicely
as he could
to leave him
    alone.

Wherever you are,
  Helena is sure
    to follow.

And
the sliding
glass door opened,
and Helena
told us,
  Hello.

  And there,
  outside,
  he told us

    how much
  he had
  been trying
    to keep it
      all together.

For himself.
For *everyone.*

The Nightmares,

he told me,
never really
went away.

It's just
that he

had gotten
better

at hiding them.

The thought
of turning
to drinking
or drugs again
was both

a dream

and

a nightmare.

Simon
just wanted

to run.

And I
just wanted
him

to stay.

I started
to tell him.

But then:

171

Our Sister

told us
how long
she had
been waiting
for the day
where she could leave
and get away
from all of this.

Our sister
apologized
for not telling us
sooner.

Our sister
told us
how much
she missed
the days
when we
were kids.

We used to be
         best friends!
What happened
         to all of us?

It killed her
that those days
were long gone.

Cheers

ERUPTED
from inside
the house.

We all looked
          at each other
          as we
          stood out there
                         shivering
          in the chilly
November air.

We knew
exactly
what those
cheers meant.

And it was
the most
                amazing sound.

It suddenly
became *too cold*.

                    And we ran
                         for the door.

Twelve Votes!

My grandpa laughed
as streamers
flew around us.

It became
a full-blown party.

And then
it hit me.

My dad.
Dr. Knights.

Now
the KING
of the
        entire suburb.

Twelve votes
is all
it took.

We did it!

        We did it?!

God
help us all.

No Time

to get used
to changes
all over again.

No time
for Dad
> *to even*
> *breathe*
as his
four-year
term
began.

No time
> to prepare
> for our
> 18th birthday
> or what home
> would be like
> *without Helena.*

But, hey.
I would be
done with school
in no time.
> And maybe I,
> Henry Knights,
> would go on
> to do
> > *great things.*

Not Enough Time

in the weeks
that followed
to say goodbye
to Simon
as he got ready
to leave
for California.

Grandma Knights
promised us
he would be
in good hands.

I felt like
he was
leaving for war
all over again.

And Gracie Lyn
was a mess.

Simon Asked

Gracie Lyn
to take Clara Rose
and come with him
for just a month
or two.

But Gracie Lyn
begged Simon
to stay home.

And find
a better doctor
here.

Her job.
Her friends.
And us.
       Everything
       was here.

She understood
that he needed
the help
       and I know
       she felt terrible
telling Simon
that he was asking

too much.

On Our Birthday

Helena and I
blew out
18 candles
on our cake.

And my dad
whispered something
to Simon
and Gracie Lyn.

They both
disappeared
for a moment
and returned
with two envelopes;
one in each
of their hands.

My dad
smiled
and told us:

Happy eighteenth birthday.
We love you.

Simon
handed me an envelope.
              Gracie Lyn handed
                    Helena the other.

It Had Taken

my dad
and Simon
and Gracie Lyn
             months
             of searching.

It had taken
every tool
        and website
and hour
imaginable
                to find
                what my
                sister and I

needed
to see.

Wanted to see.

It was
the birthday gift
to end
all birthday gifts.

They had found
our mother.

Days Later

Helena and I
finally
gathered the courage
to make
that first phone call.

Simon
and my dad
offered
to be there
when me
and Helena
decided to call.

           And we agreed.

The phone
seemed to ring
forever.

And then
suddenly,
the face
of our mother
appeared
on the screen
of Helena's phone.

And with a smile,
she gently said:

Hey, you two!

Our Mother

was *beautiful*.

I could tell
she was tired
and sad
and excited
all at the same time.

(So were we.)

She smiled.
And she cried.

Her voice
was warm.

And welcoming.

She had
the same
red-orange hair
that I shared
with my sister.

She told us
how she
cleaned up
her life a few
years after Helena
and I

were taken away.
And
how she
saved up
her money
to go to school
and become
a nurse.

Our mother
married only once,
and we had
a half-sister
that was
excited
to learn about us.

My mother
was born
and raised
in Illinois.

She never left.

And
our mother
was happy
knowing
that her twins
ended up
with such
a good family.

We Were All

packed up
just a few
short weeks later.

Helena and I
were taking
the weekend
to make the
16-hour drive
to Bloomington, Illinois.

And Simon
was hours away
from getting on his
eight-hour flight
to California.

We were all
prepared
to leave

but I know
that *none of us*

were actually

ready.

Suddenly

all of us
were having
second thoughts.

My dad
was an
emotional
train wreck.

And I told him:

*Helena and I
will be back
on Monday!*

> And don't
> even get me
> started
> on Gracie Lyn.

That girl
was a mess.

But
there's actually
a very good
reason for that.

Because
suddenly,

my brother
called everybody
into the living room.

And suddenly
our lives
were about to get
a whole lot
more interesting.

There Was

this look
of pleasant shock
on Simon's face.

And this sort
of sparkle
in Gracie Lyn's
eyes.

It was

the same
exact look
that they had

when Gracie Lyn
first showed up
at our door
with Clara Rose.

That Afternoon

I asked Simon
in the garage
if he was scared
becoming a father
for a second time.

He nodded his head
with a smile.

And then
he asked me:

> *You and Helena*
> *are coming back,*
> *right?*

And I replied:

What?
And miss all this?

> *Are you*
> *coming back*
> *after California?*

> And
> Simon said:

> *Of course.*
> *Knight's Honor.*

> *What about*
> *after you graduate?*

Maybe college,
        like Helena.

Or maybe
the police academy,
        like Matthew.

                Simon
                wrinkled his nose.

                        Really?
                        After what they
                                put me—
                                and us!—through?

Well,
we didn't exactly
make it easy on them,

I said.

                And then,
                Simon thought about it
                        some more.

                And he smirked.

                Officer Knights, though.

Has a nice
        ring to it.

                        And you'd
                                be great.

Our Dad

came into
the garage, saying:

Oh! I'm glad
> *you're both out here!*

He thanked us
for standing by him
and *each other*
these past
few months.

We thanked him
for putting up
with us.

The pranks.
> *The headaches.*
For being
> *a good dad.*

And then,
I thanked them *both*
for finding
my
mother.

> And my dad said:

No Matter

how bad
things might get,

how badly
you mess up,

or how much
trouble
you find
yourself in,

remember:
I am your dad.

And I
always will be.

My Dad Explained

how Grandpa Knights
wanted him
to run
   for *mayor*
     next November.

And they
were *so excited*
that everyone
would be here.

   To help out.

Oh,
great,
     Simon and I said.

Our dad
hugged us
   before going back
   inside.

We both
stood there
for a minute
    in stunned silence.

The Doorbell Rang

and Simon
excitedly
rushed me
back into the house.

At the front door
was my sister
calling for my dad.

And standing
on the porch
was my dad's
last girlfriend,
from last year.

                  With a baby
                      in her arms.

      I heard
      my brother
      in the kitchen,
      trying *so hard*
      to contain
      his laughter

            as my dad
            awkwardly
                greeted her.

                  Our first
                  prank together
                  went exactly
                  as planned.

WANT TO KEEP READING?

If you liked this book, check out another book

from West 44 Books:

AND WE CALL IT LOVE

BY AMANDA VINK

ISBN: 9781538382752

Zari

Love Is

dedication,
responsibility,
success.

Love is
always doing
your best.

Love is
coming out on top
when put to the test.

Check out more books at:
www.west44books.com

An imprint of Enslow Publishing

WEST 44 BOOKS™

ABOUT THE AUTHOR

P.A. Kurch first began Knights of Suburbia as a comic strip in his college newspaper that was largely based on his own experiences of his older brother's deployment in Iraq and Afghanistan. He is excited to finally be able to share this story with readers as his first officially published work. When he is not writing or drawing, P.A. Kurch gets to be the biggest kid-at-heart every day as a teacher.